MORGAN'S SURPRISE

JAYNE RYLON

eBook ISBN: 978-1-941785-29-4
Print ISBN: 978-1-941785-57-7

Ebook Cover Art By Angela Waters
Print Book Cover Art By Jayne Rylon
Interior Print Book Design By Jayne Rylon

Sign Up For The Naughty News!
Contests, sneak peeks, appearance info, and more.
www.jaynerylon.com/newsletter

Shop
Autographed books, reading-themed apparel, notebooks, totes, and more.
www.jaynerylon.com/shop

Contact Jayne
Email: contact@jaynerylon.com
Website: www.jaynerylon.com
Facebook: Facebook.com/JayneRylon
Twitter: @JayneRylon

OTHER BOOKS BY JAYNE RYLON

DIVEMASTERS
Going Down
Going Deep
Going Hard

MEN IN BLUE
Night is Darkest
Razor's Edge
Mistress's Master
Spread Your Wings
Wounded Hearts
Bound For You

POWERTOOLS
Kate's Crew
Morgan's Surprise
Kayla's Gift
Devon's Pair
Nailed to the Wall
Hammer it Home

HOTRODS
King Cobra
Mustang Sally
Super Nova
Rebel on the Run
Swinger Style
Barracuda's Heart
Touch of Amber
Long Time Coming

COMPASS BROTHERS
Northern Exposure
Southern Comfort
Eastern Ambitions
Western Ties

COMPASS GIRLS
Winter's Thaw
Hope Springs
Summer Fling
Falling Softly

PLAY DOCTOR
Dream Machine
Healing Touch

DEDICATION

As always, this one is for you the reader.

CHAPTER ONE

Morgan aimed a puff of breath at the flame dancing on top of the candle.

"Wait! Too fast! Didn't you make a wish first?" Kate jerked the plate holding Morgan's cupcake out of the trajectory of the warm air. The orange glow dimmed but didn't extinguish. "There must be something you want."

Carnal visions burned hotter than the fire melting the sprinkle-coated frosting of her gourmet confection into a golden pool. The color reminded Morgan of the burnished skin of her crush. It should be illegal for Joe to gallivant without a shirt on as often as he did. Spectacular memories of his displays sparked her fantasies at the most inopportune moments of the day and wreaked havoc on her sleep patterns.

Kate was polite enough not to hound her while she let her gaze wander, devouring the glistening expanse of Joe's perfect shoulders. Morgan sighed when she thought about the painted wooden sign he'd crafted—and now hung—outside the plate-glass window of her fledgling bakery. It bore the name he'd helped her brainstorm. Sweet Treats.

So thoughtful. And sexy as hell.

It kind of surprised her not to see steam rolling off his bunched muscles. How could he be comfortable working half-naked in the brisk autumn air? She shook her head. The motion didn't erase all the naughty ideas sabotaging her rationality. The dirty thoughts tempted her with a variety of ways to warm the handyman up when he finished his task and rejoined them inside.

Morgan sighed when a snap of fingers returned her attention to the interior of her admittedly cute shop. It'd taken six months to decorate everything just so.

"You going to pick something...maybe someone? Or are you planning to wait until wax drips all over your birthday cupcake?" Kate chuckled.

Morgan decided denying her infatuation with Joe would be futile. Kate had been her best friend since grade school. The lucky bitch had referred the hunky craftsman and his crew of skilled friends in the peak of the summer heat—after she'd scored the crew's foreman for herself.

No way could Kate miss Morgan's similar craving.

The crew had taken on odd jobs, fixing up the crummy space in the strip mall that housed Morgan's boutique in exchange for loads of the decadent goodies she whipped up. Damn, those guys could eat. She wondered if manual labor accounted for all of the voracious appetite they possessed. It had to take more than swinging a hammer to burn off those calories. Lord knew they found some way to stay fit and trim.

She'd baked Joe's favorite today—a caramel apple tart. He deserved that and more for his considerate gesture. Two customers had already stopped in to say the colorful sign had caught their eye. Thanks to him, she'd sold out of brownies and cheesecake long before the after-work rush. Too bad she couldn't generate the nerve to offer him something a little more sinful than her luscious dessert as a reward.

She'd considered it once or twice before, but she couldn't stop drooling long enough to try. Always quick to flash his toned abs and rock solid biceps, Joe kept her off balance and lost in a haze of unvented desire. He'd become her favorite treat weeks ago. An instant addiction. Thoughts of him left her craving a taste—or more—of him in the dead of night.

She bit her lip when he reached for something along the roofline. From his perch on the ladder, his body rippled with strength.

"Damn, Kate. I don't think the birthday fairy would sanction what I have in mind." Morgan grimaced at the dopey grin on her friend's face. Three months of blissful dating and wild nights with her boyfriend, Mike, had turned the woman into a ridiculous ball of giggles with a perma-smile. Worse were the googly eyes that emerged when the love of her life entered the room. Kate and Mike's soul-deep bond was hell to be around.

Jealousy didn't exactly flatter a girl.

"The big 3-0's not until the weekend anyway." Morgan pried her stare from Joe.

"I know but Mike and I will be out of town then, so it counts today. Besides, you'll never know if you don't try." Kate squeezed Morgan's hand. "Sometimes dreams come true. Believe me."

Yep. There went that grin again. "Your face is going to stick like that if you're not careful."

Kate kept right on beaming.

Morgan swallowed hard then scrunched her eyes closed. She was tired of hoping Joe would ask her out. So she tried a new tactic instead.

I wish I had the courage to ask him on a date. It's time to move on. Time to try again. I wish I could take a risk—be wild for once in my life.

When she blinked into the amber autumn light streaming through the window, Joe had vanished. A cosmic sign? Or had he needed some extra tool off his pickup?

"So... Was Joe the only guy involved in that wish or did some of the other hot construction workers we know feature in it too?"

Morgan's mouth gaped open. More than Joe?

She never would have confessed to greed that titanic on her own, but Kate knew her better than anyone. Morgan had thought about it. A lot. The way the guys worked seamlessly together on projects made their bond impossible to ignore. When they'd crowded upstairs—in her tiny apartment over the bakery—for beer and cookies, they'd overflowed the cramped space with testosterone and something a bit more elusive.

Their camaraderie transcended their partnership. At least she thought it did. But she could have imagined the inside jokes, meaningful looks and secret smiles more common between lovers than friends.

The men's intimacy could have been a figment of her overactive imagination but there was no mistaking their open arms. They'd accepted her right away, making her more than just a friend of a friend. Every time Morgan witnessed the interplay between the partners, her mind had spun with possibilities. That didn't mean she had to say so. "Isn't it one of the cardinal rules of wishing—if you tell, it won't come true?"

"Come on, you don't believe that nonsense do you?" Kate joked but persisted with a wiggle of her brows. "Fess up. You've wondered what it would be like to have them in your bed. At the very minimum, you're burning up the sheets with Joe in your dreams."

"Okay, fine. How could any woman resist? They're buff, hardworking, playful, sexy as sin and sweet. I've got it bad for Joe. So damn bad. Like, worse than our Bon Jovi lust in high school bad. He's strong but gentle. I could talk to him for days. He's always surprising me with little things that make my day. And the way he fills out those ripped jeans has me thinking I'm going into cardiac arrest every time he bends over. But the rest of the crew isn't far behind. Hell I'm so distracted, I've burnt more cookies since they've come around than in all the rest of my life."

"About time you admitted it."

Morgan's heart froze at the deep rumble over her shoulder. It kicked in triple time when a broad hand settled on the side of her neck. She jerked from the retro-dinette chair she and Joe had salvaged and restored last weekend.

The sneaky bastard caught the vinyl-covered seat, saving it from crashing to the floor. Would he do the same for her if her jellied knees gave out?

"You set me up." She gaped at Kate, betrayal and humiliation burning her cheeks.

"No, I'm sorry." Her best friend stood, reaching out, but Morgan scooted further into the corner to avoid her seeking grasp. "I didn't know he was there. I swear."

"I came through the kitchen. Left my boots out back so I wouldn't track mud all over the place." Joe waved toward his socks. His grin turned feral. "But I won't pretend to be sorry about what I heard. You want me. Bad."

"Jerk!"

"Maybe. But only because I've let this shit go on too long." He scrubbed his hands over his eyes. "You're so skittish. I planned to take things slow. I thought if I didn't pressure you, you'd get comfortable with me. With the guys. I didn't want to chance things. Didn't want you to run."

"Tell him why, Morgan." Kate's soft advice rankled. "Tell him about—"

"Hell, no. Not now. Not after this." Morgan's hands flailed in the air. Her glare whipped between her best friend and the stud she'd made a fool of herself over.

"Kate, maybe it'd be best if you did a little sharing of your own."

Joe had never used that stern tone in Morgan's presence before. She hated how it dampened her panties when she wanted nothing more than to escape. It wasn't as if she could take back her declaration. Upstairs, she could lick her wounds. Maybe in a year or five she could show her face around her friends again.

"I..." The other woman attempted to speak but had to clear her throat and start over. Twice.

Her hesitation glued Morgan's sneakers to the floor.

"You have nothing to be ashamed of, Kate. Neither of you do." Joe stroked her friend's hair.

Morgan had to swallow the acrid burn of envy.

Kate nodded. "When Mike and I first started dating, I told him about a fantasy of mine. I wondered what it would be like to have more than one man as a lover. At the same time. The crew granted my wish. They shared themselves with me. And Mike."

Holy crap. Had Morgan heard that right? "You mean..."

"Yeah, cupcake. The six of us had a smoking affair. One hell of a pool party." Joe's gorgeous green eyes went glassy as he remembered. "I'm not going to lie, the crew has messed around before. With other ladies...and sometimes by ourselves."

The proud set of his jaw, as if he prepared for a blow, ticked her off. Couldn't he tell how much the revelation turned her on? She'd swear her nipples were about to poke through her shirt, and her thighs trembled. This time the reaction had nothing to do with fear.

"You expect me to run screaming? Rant at you?" How many women had rejected him after finding out about his sexual proclivities?

"Maybe." He shrugged then leaned against the counter, his shoulders relaxing.

"It's not something you learn about your friends every day." Kate winced when Morgan turned her attention toward her.

"How can you think I'd judge you? You've always been there for me." Morgan tilted her head as she studied her friend. "If anything, I'm upgrading your status from lucky bitch to queen of all lucky bitches. Damn you for not spilling the details right away. What's the use in having a best friend if she doesn't come running to gloat about five of the sexiest men on the planet ravishing her?"

Kate beamed as she lunged across the gap between them and threw her arms around Morgan.

"But...one question." She sensed both Joe and Kate holding their breath as she tried to rein in her disappointment enough to keep it from coloring her tone. "Why twist my arm about how much I want Joe—"

A growl startled her into meeting his forest green eyes.

"—if you already have dibs? Shit, I didn't mean to step on any toes." Her stomach lurched at the thought of damaging her dearest friendship.

"I think you should field this one." Kate held her palms out toward Joe.

He paused for several seconds before speaking. "It's not like that between us. I mean, we all knew Mike was serious about Kate. Never seen him mope around like a lost puppy before. I laughed when she had him chasing his tail for months. Maybe that's why I'm gettin' some of my own damn medicine lately."

Kate giggled. "Mike's enjoyed the payback for sure."

"When things started heating up between them, he came to the crew. Told us about her request. I can't explain what it's like with the guys. I'm not great with words. But I can say we're closer than brothers. Comfortable with each other—with what each of us needs and what our limits are. That doesn't mean we're in some kind of relationship though. Except for James and Neil. They *are* pretty much a pair for life. Man, this is clear as mud, I'm sure."

Morgan didn't realize she'd moved until her fingers rested on his tensed forearm. Explaining didn't come easy. The corner of his mouth tipped up at the contact.

"I guess the bottom line is we respect each other. Kate's one of us now. It doesn't mean anything beyond that, though. We're all adults. I may not be the sharpest tool in the shed, but I see her and Mike are in this for the long haul. If they want to share some of their joy with the rest of us then we'd be glad to join in. If not, we get that too."

"The guys in the crew see other people all the time." Kate shot her a poignant stare.

It was now or never. Morgan drew a deep breath then prayed birthday magic could work in her favor. Just this once. "So… If I asked you to check out the autumn festival with me tomorrow night—"

"I'd do this." Joe wrapped her in the heat of his muscles and squeezed her tight. He dropped a kiss on the tip of her nose before teasing the seam of her lips. She parted for him, but he didn't delve inside. Not now. Not with Kate staring at them, her hands clasped in front of her, standing on tiptoes, her eyes wide.

But the lingering tingle Joe's lips had inspired promised much, much more to come.

Morgan groaned then licked the spot he'd singed with his caress. Mmm… "You've been stealing cookies off the cooling racks again."

Somehow the Belgian chocolate she'd used in them tasted better after mixing with Joe.

"I'll make it up to you." The power of his grin caused her stomach to do flip-flops. "Tomorrow night. I'll pick you up at the bakery's booth around seven."

"Who'll take care of—?"

"Let me worry about the details. You like my surprises, remember? I guarantee you'll have a good time."

Morgan tried to convince herself she'd be satisfied with some mulled cider and a run through the infamous corn maze with this gorgeous man by her side. But when he patted her ass on the way out, she swore she wouldn't settle for less than a very naughty hayride.

CHAPTER TWO

"You kids have a good time. And don't do anything we wouldn't do." Mike and Kate shooed them from the bakery stand with a wink and a nod.

"I understand if you don't want to leave." Joe turned to Morgan after measuring the line of customers. It stretched out the entrance of the old barn that housed vendors at the annual festival. He didn't blame the hungry crowd. The assortment of sweet creations looked almost as tasty as his date. Almost.

"No. Let's get out of here while we can. The store will sell out soon. The last of the stock I brought is on display now."

"Congratulations. I knew it wouldn't be long before the rest of the town caught on."

"Thanks." Her megawatt smile flanked by killer dimples stole his breath. The rare glimpse made him feel like a photographer on safari who captured never-before-seen wildlife behavior. Maybe now that things were looking up with her business, Morgan could learn to smile more. "Besides, Kate owes me for yesterday."

"I'm pretty sure *I* owe *her*."

Morgan cleared her throat and adjusted the hem of her light brown sweater over the seam of her faded jeans. He wondered if the fuzzy fabric was as ultra-soft as it looked. With any luck, he'd find out for himself before the night ended.

A rambunctious toddler veered into their path when she escaped from her harried mother. Joe cupped his hand around Morgan's elbow and steered her out of the chaos. Yep. The sweater caressed his palm, tempting him to burrow beneath it to the warm flesh inside.

Damn, he was screwed. He'd planned to take things slow, but weeks of keeping his distance threatened his restraint. He forced his grip to relax, afraid of spooking her again.

"Everything okay?" Morgan's cherry-scented breath tickled the side of his neck as she leaned closer to speak over the din of the throng and the music belting out of the local radio station's amplifiers.

"Uh...yeah." He stifled a groan. "Hoping you like what I have planned."

"Planned?" She tilted her head then peeked up at him from beneath the long, dark lashes that emphasized her gorgeous, dove-grey eyes. "I thought we were going to hang out at the festival?"

"Something like that." Joe grinned at the anticipation in her glance. He loved delighting her with little things and hoped she'd react as well to what he had in store for their evening. The way she lit up shifted something in his gut. And made him wonder about the man she'd nearly married last year. What kind of damage had that asshole inflicted?

Kate had refused to give him details no matter how hard he'd pressed, but it was clear the prick had hurt Morgan. Deeply. He intended to try his best to erase the sadness he'd sensed lingering inside her—hoped she'd let him be more than a rebound guy. But he'd settle for healing if he had to. If he could. It infuriated him to see such an amazing woman hiding from the world and herself.

One step at a time, buddy.

"How about we start with a hay ride?"

***

Oh crap! Morgan blushed at the suggestion. Had Joe plucked the dirty thought from her mind yesterday? If she were so transparent, why would he pursue her instead of shoving her away like Craig had when he'd finally realized all she desired?

"Are you allergic to hay or something?"

She hadn't realized she'd stopped dead in her tracks until the pressure of his warm fingers singed the back of her arm.

"Uh, no. Sorry." Morgan studied the tiny scuff on the toe of her black leather boots. She hadn't worn them in quite a while, but the extra height afforded by the stiletto heels eliminated some of the disparity between her and Joe. In the commotion of preparation for the festival, she hadn't had time to search for polish.

"Why do I make you so uncomfortable?" His tense tone drew her gaze to his handsome, if rugged, face. The corners of his plump lips pinched together as though he hadn't meant to speak aloud. "I would never do anything you don't want. But, if you're more comfortable staying around here that's fine too."

Morgan couldn't stop herself from turning into the solid bulk of his chest and giving him a quick, one-armed hug. "Thanks for offering, but that's not necessary. I trust you."

Crazy but true.

She'd spent most of the summer with this man, alone as they worked on her store or surrounded by his equally burly friends. Funny how they'd never once intimidated her in the cramped space. Around them, she felt safe.

His smile answered for him as he dropped a kiss on her forehead. They resumed their leisurely pace toward the edge of the gravel lot where several tractors towing platforms, ringed with hay, waited for a full load of passengers. His knuckles stroked the sensitive space between her fingers as he held them in a loose grip.

A mix of children hopped up on candy, parents enjoying the brisk but not too chilly evening and young couples out for an evening of local entertainment piled into the wagon. Joe paused to boost a straggling kid onto the loose bales before leaping up himself. He turned and offered his hand. She gladly accepted. He tugged her into his arms as a few women nudged over to make room for his wide shoulders. When it looked like they'd run out of space, Morgan peeked toward the next wagon.

Instead of making a move in that direction, Joe settled in the gap remaining then scooped her into his lap before she could object. Not that she would have. The leather of his jacket smelled divine and quickly warmed with the heat of her cheek, pressed to the supple material. The woman to their right shot Morgan an envious grin before resuming her conversation with her friends.

The cramped space forced Morgan's hands to land against the taut muscles of Joe's chest beneath his thin T-shirt. Defined lines tempted her to trace them downward to the ridges of his abdomen, but she resisted. Barely.

"Comfortable?" He nuzzled her temple while his hands ran along the length of her spine. One settled on her knee, and the other on her waist, for several seconds before she remembered to respond with words instead of a simple purr.

"Very." Holy shit. Had that husky sigh come from her? Thank God for their chaperones or she might have been tempted to throw decorum out the window and beg Joe to touch her more intimately right here and now.

"Blanket?"

Morgan blinked up at the attendant waving a quilt in their direction.

"Sure." Joe winked when her mouth gaped into a giant O. "Wouldn't want you to catch a chill."

Between the helpful older man and her date, they bundled her under the well-worn cover in a matter of moments—right along with Joe's wandering fingers. She laughed when he traced the dip of her side beneath the hem of her sweater. Amid the banter of the other passengers, no one seemed to notice.

Her brows rose when Joe's palm cupped her ribcage, the side of his hand brushing the underside of her breast. No way could his touch be accidental. The warm hold soothed her. She relaxed further into the cushion of his thighs, chest and arms.

Joe flashed a terrible imitation of an innocent grin then proceeded to ask her questions about the new assortment she'd planned in order to capitalize on the change of seasons. They talked about the successes and failures of her recent product testing as the tractor began to pull them along the bumpy farm grounds toward the pumpkin patch.

To avoid embarrassing herself, she thought of things she had to do this week. That way she might be able to ignore the contact of their bodies shifting against each other and the hard length of Joe's denim-clad erection at her hip.

Before she left tonight, she'd snag a basketful of local produce to use in the tarts she'd unveil this week. "Do you like pumpkins? I have some new recipes I'd like to try if you don't mind being my guinea pig."

Her question came out more like a squeak.

"I'll eat anything of yours. After tonight, I have a feeling pumpkins may be my new favorite vegetable."

The children at the front of the wagon sang off-key loud enough she couldn't swear she'd heard him right.

Before she could clarify, the cart lurched to a halt.

"I think this is our stop."

"Huh?"

"We're getting out. Come on, you'll see." Joe set her on her feet as the attendant collected their cover.

"Don't forget, the last ride comes by at midnight. After that you're on your own to make it back to your cars. If they haven't turned into pumpkins by then." The man laughed at his own joke.

Joe planted one hand on the rail then leapt to the ground with a hell of a lot more grace than she could muster. He wrapped his hands around her waist then lifted her from the wagon as though she weighed about as much as a bag of confectioner's sugar.

Her body slid along every hard inch of his on the way down.

Oh my.

The man in the wagon tossed Joe a flashlight then trundled off into the dark toward the main barns they'd started at. In the wake of the raucous gathering and the sputtering diesel engine, the still night rang in her ears. Vines curled across the ground, their leaves rustling in the soft breeze.

They stood in the middle of the farm's pumpkin patch listening to each other breathe for several heartbeats.

"Okay?" Joe spoke softly but his gentle question might as well have been gunfire. It sliced through the quiet. "Your phone works out here if you want to call the cops on me for abducting you or have Mike kick my ass."

"Not necessary." She shivered a little, but it had nothing to do with fear and everything to do with the excitement of being truly alone with the man she'd been dreaming of for weeks. Her curiosity grew by the second. "What are we doing out here?"

"Right this way, you'll see." Again he took her hand, entwining their fingers. Suddenly it was enough to be here, with him, walking side by side along a slightly wider row in the field.

A beam of light swept from edge to edge, guiding Morgan out of danger of twisting an ankle in her ridiculous boots as long as she kept to her toes. The heels made her calves look fantastic, but had no place in the tilled dirt.

The row narrowed, forcing her behind Joe. She hummed when he tucked her fingers into the waistband of his jeans. So warm. But even that distance made the walk treacherous in the moonlight.

Rocks and divots in the earth waited to trip her. She stumbled a bit before her eyes adjusted after the bright white of the flashlight. Joe stopped in front of her. She plastered herself along his backside before she could reverse her momentum. Pure male strength greeted every inch of her from the hard tips of her breasts to the soft curve of her belly, which met his firm ass.

Morgan took a step away, thanking all the powers of the universe he couldn't spot her face flaming in the shadows or smell the scent of her instant arousal. Instead of continuing on, Joe crouched, holding his arms out from his sides.

"Hop on. It's not far from here but I don't want to spoil the fun before it's begun."

When she simply stood and gawked, he glanced over his shoulder.

"What, you don't like the idea of riding me?"

Jesus. It was either admit she enjoyed the thought all too much or pretend her panties hadn't drenched at their collision and his naughty implication. Without another objection, she climbed onboard.

The powerful shift of his torso between her thighs had her groaning before she could prevent the sound from escaping. His fingers stroked the back of her knees. The motion, designed to soothe, instigated a hormonal riot of massive proportions.

"Too fast?" Joe slowed to a pace that jostled her less but caressed her core with each tread of his long stride.

She didn't attempt to answer. Clinging tighter to his sculpted chest, laying her head on his solid shoulder and surrendering to her hunger before it raged out of control seemed wiser. Her lips brushed his neck with each step, but sensory overload prevented her from fidgeting. If she moved her head, her rock-hard nipples would stroke his shoulder blades. If she adjusted her hips, her steaming pussy would graze his lower back.

Why was that a bad idea again?

Her tongue nipped out to taste Joe's nape. Salty spice and oak. He cleared his throat. Could she make it hard for him to speak too?

God she hoped so.

"We're here." He released her thighs slow enough she had time to ensure her footing despite her wobbly legs. She relinquished her hold on him one finger at a time. Too bad their destination hadn't been another five miles, or five hundred, away.

Joe turned to face her, blocking the view behind him. He took her hands in his, his thumbs brushing the sensitive centers of her palms. Then he lifted them over her eyes. "Don't peek. Give me a minute, okay?"

"Would now be a good time to tell you the dark isn't my favorite thing?"

"I'll be right here." The deep timbre of his voice continued to croon to her as he moved to the left then the right, a little further away then close again, so she never felt alone.

A whoosh carried to her ears a moment before heat and orange light washed over her cheeks.

"Can I look now?"

"Sure." His breath teased her face as he took his place behind her, wrapping an arm around her waist and drawing her back against his chest.

Morgan peeked between her fingers. "Holy crap!"

The digits slammed closed once more. That couldn't have been what it looked like. She must be dreaming again. But when she opened her eyes, his surprise hadn't vanished. Her jaw hung open far enough to swallow a handful of bugs. Fortunately, the brisk air kept them away.

"Is that a good holy crap or a bad holy crap?"

She couldn't answer immediately. A knot as big as a squash grew in her throat as she scanned the small pavilion sheltering them from the chill. A fire pit blazed in the center of the space, perfuming the air with the scent of applewood from the neighboring orchard.

Carved pumpkin lanterns of every size and shape ringed the perimeter of the cement-slab floor, hung from wires over the rafters and perched on sporadic wooden pillars. A few more made an elaborate centerpiece for the picnic table, laden with Indian corn, gourds, cider and other autumn treats. Geometric shapes glowed and bobbed with the radiance of the tea lights within. Warmth and welcome washed the entire space.

"You did all this for me?" She studied one of the beautiful designs so he couldn't see the sheen of moisture in her eyes.

"I did it for us," he whispered into her ear a moment before he cupped her chin in his fingers then angled her jaw until she couldn't avoid the sincerity in his gaze. "I wanted our first time together to be special. As special for you as I know it will be for me."

CHAPTER THREE

"First time?" Morgan didn't object, really. She'd lusted after the man for weeks, but she hadn't expected him to put it all on the line like that. Or to make the molten desire flowing between them so personal. Why couldn't she be more like him?

"Shit. I didn't mean that like it sounded, cupcake. I meant our first date, our first intimate conversation, our first dinner. Maybe our first real kiss." When she still didn't say anything, he sputtered. "Unless... I mean, I want you Morgan. Whatever you'll take from me is yours. I hoped, but never think I assumed."

"God, how do you do that?"

"Put my foot in my mouth? It's pretty easy." He laughed. "I have a lot of practice."

"No. You distill complicated issues to their essence. I would have worried for three days about how to say what you just did—and probably would have bungled it anyway or lost my nerve—but you follow your instincts and they never lead you wrong. I really admire that about you, Joe."

"I'm a simple man." He scrubbed his hands over his cheeks. Were they red from the fire, or from her praise?

"You're exactly the kind of man I like. Direct. Honest without being harsh. Strong and generous. They're all great qualities." She smiled. "I never have to guess with you."

"Again, is that a good thing?"

She crossed the gap between them and kissed his cheek before she started bawling. "It's a really good thing. Thank you. For everything. This has already been one of the most amazing nights of my life."

"And what firsts would you like to try to make it even better?"

"Can we see where things go?"

"Yeah. Of course." His smile returned, bigger than before. "How about we start with dinner?"

Her stomach growled in response. "Sounds good to me."

They both laughed as they tucked into the fixed bench of the picnic table, draped in black linen. Joe straddled the plank, seating himself on her right so that he faced her. His left hand stroked her hair and he stole a peck on her cheek before admitting, "Kate and the rest of the crew helped me organize everything. The guys know you're like a sister to Kate, and they're all happy we're finally doing something about—"

He gestured between himself and her.

"They said that?" She watched as he dipped mulled cider from the warmer into her mug. Cinnamon and cloves mixed with the leather of Joe's jacket, nearly making her high from the delicious scents surrounding her.

"They didn't have to." Joe tucked a strand of hair behind her ear. "I can tell by the way they act around you and how much they've ripped on me for waiting to ask you out."

"What if they didn't approve of me?"

Joe waited until he'd finished plating several slices of fresh apples drizzled with caramel, a mixture of nuts and something that looked like herbed chicken with eggplant and other seasonal vegetables from the insulated bag on the table.

"Look, Morgan. I realize what Kate told you the other day could be confusing. I'm not sure I understand it myself. There aren't any hard and fast laws when it comes to the crew and the women we've entertained." Joe trailed one finger across the corner of her mouth, where a stray bit of foam from their drinks had landed. He brought the digit to his lips and licked it clean. "Let's make one thing clear, though. If the crew had been crazy enough not to care about you like I do, I still wouldn't have walked away. I couldn't have."

Her stomach clenched at his assertion. Almost as hard as when he sucked her taste from his fingertip. Desire coursed through her as she imagined his tongue lapping at her juices with such gusto. And what if it were more than just Joe devouring her? Could she handle three other men as potent and masculine as him? Would he still want her if she couldn't?

"What happens between us is between us. Anything else we decide to do or not do can come later. But, I am curious. You didn't say much yesterday. How do you feel about what Kate told you?"

"It's hot!" She clapped her hand over her mouth in horror. She had *not* blurted that in the middle of their heart to heart.

Joe laughed, then forked up a piece of chicken. He cupped his hand beneath the chunk of steaming meat and guided it to her mouth. She gathered her thoughts as she chewed. The savory dish delighted her taste buds.

"Mmm. This is great."

"Do you know how rough it is to cook for a chef? I got my balls in a bunch trying to pick the perfect thing."

"I'd say you did fine. Better than." She swallowed another draught of cider then bit the bullet. She could be as brave as her date. "And, yes, I'm completely turned on by the idea of the crew but it scares me too. I don't want you to think I'm a slut. I, um, care too much about you to ruin this for one night of fun."

"Morgan." He set his mug on the table hard enough to make the candles shimmer. "That's bullshit. Is that what you think? That enjoying a ménage with people who know you and respect you is the same as sleeping with any man who needs to get off? If it is, then this isn't for you."

"Damn, now I offended you." She bit her lip. "I only meant that sometimes men don't know what they want. A fantasy that sounds hot in theory can change the way someone looks at you afterward. It can kill a good thing. I don't want to take that risk."

Her lip trembled.

"Hey, hey. Sorry. I didn't mean to upset you." Joe petted her arm. His gorgeous green eyes closed to a slit. "Is that what happened with your ex? Did that douche offer to make your dreams come true then punish you for them once he'd gotten his rocks off?"

She focused on savoring the delicious meal Joe had slaved over. Anything was better than letting it go to waste. Because if she thought about Craig, everything would taste like cardboard.

"He did." Joe scooted closer until the heat of his thighs bracketed her. "That bastard."

Morgan set her silverware on her plate when he enfolded her in his embrace. He covered her face with butterfly kisses though his legs quivered with pent-up fury.

"Yeah, he sort of planted an idea in my head. He wanted me to try a threesome with another woman. I went along with it. No, that sounds like I didn't want to experiment. I was curious, and I liked it. She was soft and lush. So different from a man. It just wasn't what I want all the time."

"Holy shit, that's hot."

"Yeah, but he'd promised to try a threesome with another man if I did it with another woman. Only he never came through. He told me it was wrong to want to be with someone else if we were in love. He dumped me and asked me to return his ring."

"What a selfish asshole."

"Something like that. Actually, he decided he liked her better. They're together now. I saw them in the grocery store not long after. She was wearing my diamond. Some of my old friends told me they're living with another woman. I was lucky, really. Everything fell apart before we actually got married, had a house or kids. Before I was too invested."

"That would never happen with me, Morgan." Joe cradled her against his heaving chest. "I'd love every minute of making your dreams come true. And I sure as hell wouldn't change my mind in the light of day. I would expect the same acceptance from my partner. God knows I've done things a lot of women wouldn't condone."

"You mean fooling around with the rest of the crew?"

"Yeah." He looked straight into her eyes. "I've enjoyed sex with them. I've touched them, been touched, even tried fucking James once but it wasn't really my thing. Don't get me wrong. It was hot. And I don't respect his lifestyle any less. Like you said, just not what I want most times."

She swallowed hard as she imagined the two men together. The raw power and grace they both possessed would have been amazing to see unleashed. She moaned.

Joe laughed. "Glad to know that doesn't repulse you."

"Exactly the opposite. So what *do* you want most times?"

"A woman who's honest and open with her needs. Someone who makes me laugh, who gets me. I'm not rich or a genius, but I'll never let you down. I want someone who'll be there for me like that. Someone I can work through the tough times with. No matter what else we do or don't do together."

Morgan couldn't wait one more second. It was as though he'd stolen the words straight from her soul. She leaned into his hold, wrapped her hand around the nape of his neck and dragged him to her for a scorching kiss. Their lips sealed like pieces in a matched set. She tasted the spice and sweetness of their meal as it mingled with his unique flavor.

If she could extract his scrumptiousness and bottle it for her recipes, she'd be set for life.

Joe shifted and, for a moment, she thought he intended to pull away.

"No, stay."

"Not going anywhere without you. We'll be more comfortable over there." He jerked his head toward the opposite side of the fire pit. Black canvas had been strung up on three sides, affording some privacy—though the deserted field posed no threat except maybe from a curious deer—while still allowing the light and heat from the fire pit to stream through.

"But you worked so hard on this dinner." The idea of squandering his thoughtfulness warred with her ravenous appetite for his touch.

"Sometimes I like to eat dessert before the main course." He bit her lip then plucked her from the bench. "You know I have a huge sweet tooth."

"Is that what you're calling it these days?" She laughed at the temporary surprise in his eyes. Hell, she shocked herself with the liberation he inspired. Almost like her old self.

"Oh yeah, let me show you."

CHAPTER FOUR

Morgan wrapped her legs around Joe's waist, this time indulging in his hard length tucked against her core. He walked them backward while she devoured his mouth and speared her fingers into the thick mess of his hair, which he kept long enough to dust his shoulders.

When he entered the screened area and tipped forward, she expected her ass to meet the cool, firm floor or maybe hard-packed dirt. Instead, she sank into a decadent pile of blankets topping a plush feather mattress. More pumpkin lanterns ringed the warm nest, each bearing heart carvings she took a moment to admire despite the flames licking her insides.

Joe stripped his jacket from his shoulders then kicked off his boots. She followed his example, or would have, but he stopped her from yanking her sweater over her head with a light touch.

"Let me, sweetheart. Please." His lusty gaze raked her from head to toe. "I've thought about this moment a million times."

How could she resist? Her hands fell to her sides as she submitted to his whims, melting a little more each instant he lingered over her.

"Yes, like that. I'll take care of you." Joe unzipped her boots then slipped them from her feet before tossing them to the side to join his discarded coat. The sure massage of his fingers on her sore arches had her writhing before long.

He tugged back a corner of the plush duvet then urged her to burrow underneath. "Should be nice and toasty in there. Dave helped me rig a heated mattress pad to an old car battery. He's good at wiring shit like that. I'm pretty sure it won't electrocute us."

She laughed. "That'd be my luck. Oh well, at least whoever found us would know we went happy."

"You have no idea." Joe beamed as he tucked her under the downy covers. He traced her cheekbone then twirled her hair around his fingers.

Morgan held her breath as he stripped off his T-shirt. Air escaped with a rush when he unbuttoned his jeans. Her wide-eyed stare flicked between his hardening nipples and the smoky trail leading from the base of his washboard abs straight into the gaping vee of his fly. He toed off his socks, revealing his sexy feet, then he met her eager gaze.

"You ready for this? It's not too late to stop."

"Don't you dare. I want you to hold me—skin on skin."

"Shit, yes." He stood to peel the denim from his toned ass and bunched thighs with one swipe of his massive hands.

She gulped.

He gave ideal male forms like David a run for their money. Tan, tan skin made her itch to lick him, to discover if he tasted like salty caramel. No puny fig leaf would do the job in covering him up either. Morgan wet her lips when his cock bobbed, thick and heavy, against his inner thigh.

"Let me in, cupcake, or there won't be much to look at. It's freaking frosty out here."

"You, cold? Impossible." She laughed then invited him to lay beside her with a sweep of her arm. "It's nice and cozy in here. I think I'm actually starting to sweat a bit."

"What can I say, seeing me naked has that affect on girls."

"And some guys," Morgan added as he collapsed beside her, tickling her as punishment.

They giggled together like children telling naughty jokes, rolling beneath the heated blankets, mussing the perfect setting. Christ, had she ever enjoyed a man in her bed this much? When their chuckles died down, Joe swallowed the dregs of her laughter in another all-consuming kiss.

There was nothing funny about the way he made out.

His tongue swept past her parted lips to explore the ridges of her gums. First soft then firm as he tensed and relaxed—thrust and retreat—the moist tip flicking over hers. Teasing. Tasting. Morgan stared into the green depths of his eyes, noticing how much darker they looked when he got turned on. Before she could get her fill, he lifted up onto his arms. "Now, about that dessert."

Joe dove beneath the covers, settling between her legs. He shouldered her thighs apart then tortured her by laying his chin on her mound while he played with her abdomen. Muscles quivered beneath his exploratory strokes. He traced the swells and dips of her midriff beneath the sweater, inching the cashmere higher and higher to make room for his lips and tongue.

By the time he'd gathered the fabric below her bra, she struggled to catch a breath. His moist lips dragged across the sensitive ridges of her ribs, exacerbating her respiratory issues. If he hesitated any longer, she would take things into her own hands and speed up the process.

Morgan's hands snuck below the covers, prepared to clutch the hem and pry her sweater free when a whisper halted her motion.

"Ever want something so bad, for so long, that when you finally get it, you're not sure what to play with first?"

"Yes!" She hadn't meant to shout but she craved him everywhere, all at once. The anticipation had her on edge. "Start by stripping me faster."

His laughter held a strangled note.

Compliance had never seemed like one of Joe's strengths, but a wash of cool air snuck through the gap in the covers, replacing his scorching touch below her breasts. He skipped along her belly, avoiding her pussy entirely even when she arched toward his skimming fingers. The infuriating man caressed her legs until he reached her feet. He slid her socks off, massaged her ankles and calves then surprised the hell out of her when he fisted his hands in the fabric behind her knees. A solid yank divested her of her pants.

Thank God she hadn't opted for her skinny jeans.

A series of nips and licks along her knees to her inner thighs marked Joe's return journey to her core. He didn't screw around when he reached her soaked thong. His fingers tucked beneath the narrow ribbons forming the sides of the delicate covering then guided the scrap of underwear off her. Molten lust bubbled inside her, flowed in her veins and from her steaming pussy.

Joe emerged from their cocoon with the silky material between his teeth. He flung it to the side with a shake of his head that ruffled his hair and made her itch to feel it between her fingers again. The sight, which should have either horrified or amused her, somehow excited her more. He could recite the phonebook and it would make her hot.

Before disappearing out of sight beneath the blanket, he paused as though he couldn't resist tasting her swollen lips again. Morgan had never really enjoyed tonsil hockey before.

Something about it had always seemed too invasive, too personal, too intimate. Kissing Joe brought new meaning to lip lock.

He fit her as if they were molded for each other, tasted like all her favorite dishes in one and somehow knew exactly where to focus his efforts to drive her past reason. He licked the inside edge of her lips, tracing her gum line. A shock of pure arousal zinged straight to her pussy.

In response, she flung out her arms, clasping him to her to encourage him to do it again. He groaned, sank closer and complied. The maneuver thrilled them both as their bare legs and abdomens pressed together for the first time. His broad shoulders overflowed her clenching hands, which marked him with tiny crescents from her nails.

"Jesus!" Joe drowned out her whimper. "You feel perfect against me. Silky, soft, curvy and warm."

His hands traveled up her sides as though on rails bolted to either edge of her torso. He gathered the sweater. "Lift up."

Obedient, she raised her arms and sat forward enough for him to guide the material beneath her then over her head. The moment he revealed her cleavage, he descended to sample her abundant breasts. Her super-structured bra helped shape her, but she'd always thought her chest one of her best features.

"I'm sorry," Joe mumbled before burying his face between the pale mounds. He sucked a patch of skin above the lacy line of her bra into his mouth. The pressure of his hold stung a bit, but also beaded her nipples beneath the confines of the padded garment.

"Why apologize? So good," she panted. "More."

He angled his face to speak against the curve of her breast. "Some women don't like to be marked."

"I'm not some women." Proof of his possession, even a temporary claim, felt like a badge of honor.

"Definitely not." He licked the pretty purple spot while his talented fingers unhooked her bra with a deft flick.

"And I don't mind being marked by you." Morgan swore he held his breath as he unwrapped her chest as if it were an elegant gift. The chilly night fluttered across her nipples, crinkling them into compact nubs. Waves of contrasting heat radiated from the man above her when he swooped in, capturing the tip of one breast between his teeth, covering the other with his calloused palm.

Shocks of arousal coursed along her nerve endings, jolting them both with her reaction. She moaned long and loud when the blazing tip of his cock left a moist trail of pre-come on her thigh. Joe thrust against her as he continued to lave her breasts, suckling in time to the arc of his hips. The motion inspired her to spread her knees wider to welcome him closer to his goal.

When she snaked one leg around his hip, the blunt head of his cock traced the wet furrow of her pussy. She had to have him inside. Now.

An outraged cry escaped her throat when he eluded the shift of her hips that would have buried him to the hilt in her clenching channel.

"Wait. Gotta grab a condom."

"No." She gripped the hair at his temples to keep him in place while she gathered her scattered thoughts long enough to convince her soon-to-be lover to stay. "I'm on the pill. Don't want any barriers between us."

"Always have safe sex." Joe shook his head as much as he could in her hold. "We never do it without a rubber."

"Then you're clean." She flashed him a grateful smile. "Like me."

"Really?" His chest crushed hers when he took great heaving breaths. "Bare. Inside you?"

"Yes." She squirmed beneath the heated pressure of his weight in an attempt to wedge her arm between them and force his cock inside. "Now. Please!"

Joe's hips rocked, notching the plump, dripping tip of his erection at her entrance. The initial contact caused her to cry out. Pleasure resonated between them at the simple connection. He cupped her cheeks in his palms then bestowed a tender kiss a moment before he began to work inside.

Morgan's breath caught in her lungs then rushed out in ragged pants.

Holy shit, he feels even bigger than he looks—and that's saying something.

Another tiny hitch out then he ground forward, stretching the clamped walls of her pussy as he spread her wetness along the swollen tissue.

"Sorry." She winced when he lodged, no more than a few inches, inside her. "It's been a while and Craig—no guy I've slept with—had nothing on you."

"You're soaked, but so tight." He withdrew, inciting panic in her fevered mind. "Don't want to hurt you."

She had to have him. "Not!"

Joe evaded her seeking lips as she tried to freeze him with a kiss.

"You're not hurting me."

"I am." At least he didn't abandon their pallet. Candlelight glinted off his skin, slick with light perspiration. "But I'll fix it. Relax."

This time the cold didn't disturb her when the blankets shifted to her waist. Nothing could have penetrated the bubble of energy surrounding them. Together, they generated enough electricity to light all the stars twinkling in the sky above them.

The man of her dreams licked his way along her belly, which rose and fell as her pussy flexed—attempting to grip the thick cock that no longer tunneled inside her. His pounding heartbeat echoed in the stiff length of flesh, making it bob and bounce near her shin.

One of his hands burrowed beneath her ass, holding a whole cheek in his palm, while two fingers of the other pressed to her dripping slit. Before she could register his intent, Joe's tongue darted out and stole a taste of the juices slicking her labia. He followed the crease of her pussy to her clit, placed a gentle kiss on the hard bundle of nerves then slipped one finger in her to the second knuckle.

"Oh, yes! Yes!" Even such minimal penetration provided some relief from the pressure building within.

But she had to have more.

Much, much more.

Morgan wrapped her hand around the back of Joe's head then drew him close while she thrust her hips, fucking his face with an abandon she'd never before possessed. He devoured her in return. His primal grunts and moans of approval rocked her, forcing his finger to plumb her depths. When it glided in and out with ease, he added a second, stretching her further. The sinful ache overwhelmed her, especially combined with the figure eight he made with his tongue around her clit.

His mouth was so talented, she didn't give a fuck how many women—or men—he'd practiced his moves on before her.

"Fuck me," she screamed as his expert manipulation drove her toward the brink. "So close."

He lifted his head long enough to grin and taunt, "I bet I can make you come in the next five seconds. I want to taste your orgasm. Hear you shatter. Feel you surrender. Finally."

Joe punctuated each desire with a lick, a thrust and a nibble. He spread his fingers where they speared inside her.

"No." She didn't mean to scratch his back like a wildcat, but she couldn't restrain herself from raking her nails over his bunched shoulders. "Want you. Want your cock. Buried deep."

"Soon." He added a devious suckling on her clit.

"No!" Her head thrashed on the pillow. She could no longer hold her neck up enough to watch him at work—her bones had liquefied. "Want to come with you."

"You will," he growled around her pulsing clit. "I promise."

She didn't believe him, but her disappointment couldn't prevent the tide rushing toward her now. It had caught her in its force and dragged her out to sea, no matter how she struggled against its hold.

"Oh! Joe!"

CHAPTER FIVE

Every muscle in her body tensed into a knot of pure ecstasy a moment before her orgasm ripped her apart. Inhibitions evaporated. Undiluted instinct took control. She writhed on the mattress, wringing pleasure from her climax until not one single drop remained untapped.

Her pussy clenched hard enough she feared she might break Joe's fingers.

Morgan trembled in the aftermath of the storm, but her lover refused to let her off so easy. He slithered up her torso until he could alternate sipping from her lips and whispering naughty reassurance. His hands roamed across the landscape of her curves—soothing, calming, comforting.

"You're unbelievable. Fucking beautiful." Another nibble on her bottom lip, this one hard enough to sting.

She moaned.

"I love that you nearly drowned me." His glistening chin slid across her jaw as he deepened their kisses, allowing her to ingest the mingled flavors of their desire. "Perfect. Gorgeous."

Morgan gasped when his cock brushed her ultra-sensitive mound.

Instead of retreating, he lifted onto a straight-locked arm and closed his hand around her wrist. While staring into her eyes, he guided her grip to his straining, flushed cock. It wedged between them, hot, satiny and ready. The protruding veins along his shaft would feel divine rubbing her from within.

Though she hadn't finished quivering from the mind-blowing rapture he'd built in her, she couldn't help fusing their bodies. After all, he deserved his reward for giving her the best orgasm of her life.

"That's right, Morgan." He aided her as she fit him to her opening. "Put me inside you. Feel how much thicker my dick is than my fingers. How much longer. Can you tell how much I want you?"

"God, yes." She jerked in response to his dirty talk. A fission of arousal sparkled along her spine when the motion embedded him further. "Fuck me, Joe."

"Have to." He grunted then drilled forward, impaling her on his shaft with ease this time. "Fuck. Gripping me tight. So sexy."

He began to move inside her, thrilling her with the novelty of being joined to a large, powerful yet gentle man. Her nails sank into his ass. She relished the flex and release of his cheeks almost as much as the resulting pistoning of his tool inside her.

Joe leaned forward to nip her neck. The love bite drove her insane. Embers of her climax rekindled, surprising the hell out of her. She'd never come more than once in an evening. Never mind back to back, following the most intense release of her life.

"You like that?" He released an evil chuckle against her jaw that proved he knew just how devastating he could be to her restraint. "Yeah, that's it. Squeeze me. You want my cock don't you, cupcake?"

"Yes." She moaned as he lifted his head to stare into her eyes.

"Tell me how much you love my cock."

"Love it!" she hollered into the night. "Fuck me."

"Like this?" He introduced his length in a slow, languid glide. His control tortured her.

"No." Morgan shook her head. "Harder."

Joe pinched her nipple, creating lightning strikes from her breast straight to her pussy. "Say it. Tell me you want me to fuck you. Rough. Deep. Fast."

He drove his hips into hers hard enough to rattle her teeth between each command. Where she'd tolerated such treatment from Craig, Joe had riled her need until it boiled her blood. Each forceful thrust escalated the rapture to a new level. Her breasts jiggled against his chest. The motion stoked the flames growing inside her, setting her ablaze. The promise of fulfillment lay within her grasp. If only he would give her more.

"Yes! Fuck me. Ride me." She moaned when he began to comply. "Take me."

She strained toward completion but he yanked his cock from her pussy. She almost broke down and cried at his abandonment. His hand strangled the base of his cock as though to keep from spewing come all over her dewy skin. The length of his shaft glistened with a mix of her cream and the pearly fluid leaking from the slit in the tip.

"Turn over." He nudged her with his free hand until she rotated. "Ass in the air. Now."

Morgan had never had sex like this before. Despite his gruff tone, his affection permeated each touch. She braced for his entry but still tipped forward beneath the driving force of the lunge that buried him to the hilt. Her hands skid beneath the pillows, providing some leverage to allow her to rock her ass toward his invading shaft.

Over and over, Joe hammered inside her. His palm settled low on her belly, the heel below her navel and his fingers curling over her clit. He tapped the hard bump with each skewering stroke until all her attention focused on the center of her arousal.

Morgan's pussy contracted further, making him work to drill to the bottom of her channel. The head of his cock tunneled to the far reaches of her body despite the increasing pressure. His flexed abs smacked her ass faster and faster.

The amplitude of his strokes increased until he exited completely then slammed back inside, reopening the ring of muscle at her entrance with each pass. Finally, she could take no more. "Joe!"

"Fuck. Yeah." He grunted as the first shimmering waves of orgasm fluttered her swollen tissue around his erection. "Hurry. Going to—"

He never finished his sentence or, if he did, she sure as hell didn't hear it. They exploded together. Morgan gripped his pulsing shaft, reveling in the splatter of his semen on her sensitized tissue. Five...no, six, spurts filled her to overflowing, each one triggering an answering convulsion in her pussy.

He jerked, roared, and then—finally—went still, blanketing her back. They collapsed onto the feather bed, too destroyed by what they'd shared to move a single muscle. Harsh breaths echoed through the night for long, contented minutes.

Morgan didn't realize she'd nearly drifted off until Joe cursed under his breath, departed her pussy then shifted onto his side next to her. She moaned softly.

"Didn't mean to crush you, cupcake. Or use you so rough."

"Felt good." She turned her head to meet his concerned gaze. "Amazing. The best of my life. All of it, the whole night."

"Mine too." When she dismissed his whisper, he gripped her chin. "That's no lie, Morgan. Something about you is different. Special."

She didn't argue when he sheltered her beneath one arm, tucked her trembling body tight to his chest, and kissed her with a tenderness that melted her heart.

***

Joe had lost track of how long they'd spent, eating dinner in bed, sharing stories and roasting marshmallows over the fire—something he'd never done in the nude before. But Morgan had just finished licking the gooey white confection from his thumb as they perched cross-legged and side by side when a quick double vibration from the general direction of his abandoned pants caught his attention.

"Son of a bitch."

"What's wrong?" He hated the alarm on Morgan's gorgeous face. For a few hours she'd lost the worry lines that usually bracketed her reddened lips and smoky, bedroom eyes.

"It's late. We missed the last ride back." Joe extracted his phone from his pocket and unlocked the screen. Sure enough, the crew had sent him a text. "The guys are waiting to take us home when you're ready."

"We're going back tonight?"

The disappointment in her roughened voice both thrilled him and made him feel like crap. He wished he could give her everything she'd ever wanted but they couldn't stay out here until dawn.

"Yeah. The fire is burning out, and the temperature is dropping by the minute. We're not going to last all night. I don't want you to catch a chill." He stroked her hair into some semblance of order, though he preferred the messy just-been-fucked look on her.

"I don't think I could ever be cold when you're near me." Morgan's genuine sweetness went straight to his chest, cramping the spot over his heart.

Joe gathered their clothes. He tugged his on with brisk efficiency then helped her dress, cursing himself for every gorgeous inch of skin he covered. The potent combination of adrenaline and bright, shiny attraction they'd maintained most of the evening began to fade, leaving her sleepy and malleable. He bundled her in the duvet, and she snuggled up to his chest, molding to his lap as he sat on their makeshift bed.

With one hand, he texted the crew. The other stroked her back. He couldn't stop touching her. She dozed by the time the guys made it to their oasis although it took less than five minutes for them to arrive.

It seemed impossible. The evening's exchange had transported him. Joe felt like he'd traveled to the other side of the world instead of the middle of a pumpkin patch. The experience had changed him as surely as if he'd gone on a voyage to some faraway place and he knew he'd never be the same.

But the moment he saw the crew, it was as if he'd never left them either. They were his home, his brothers. Dave, Neil and James approached, shoulder to shoulder, with shit-eating grins stretched across their familiar faces.

"Looks like tonight was worth the trouble." Dave pitched his voice low enough to prevent waking Morgan.

"You have no idea." Joe raised her away from his chest with a grimace. Dave stepped forward to accept her from him. A few inches shorter than Joe, Dave had always been more muscular. He held Morgan as though she were light as a feather. She mumbled something under her breath then cuddled close to his friend, seeking the heat of the other man's hold.

"Christ, I'm starting to understand." Dave's gaze held a new appreciation when he experienced the full-impact of Morgan's unqualified trust and got his first taste of the lush softness of her perfect body.

"Let me put out the fire, then we can go."

As usual, the crew worked together without much instruction necessary. They assessed what had to be done and what they could each contribute to making it happen. Joe, Neil and James doused the flames in the pit and snuffed out the candles in the lanterns. They packed the leftovers into the cooler, tossed the bag of garbage on the back of their truck then hefted the mattress, blankets and other equipment in as well. In less than five minutes, they were ready to head home.

Joe damned their efficiency.

After one last look over his shoulder, he knelt and plucked a pebble from the dirt. He dropped it into his pocket before following his friends to their truck. James climbed in the driver's seat while Neil angled toward the front passenger-side door. Joe caught a glimpse of Dave rocking Morgan in the back row of the extended cab so he joined them on the bench seat.

The dome light stirred Morgan enough that she hummed and stretched, her lips brushing Dave's neck. The sight of the two of them together pumped Joe's cock hard again in an instant. She hummed at the first taste then lifted her face for a kiss, which his friend provided obligingly.

But the moment they separated, her eyes opened. "You're not Joe. You don't taste like him. Or kiss like him."

"Neither do you." Dave beamed down into her sultry eyes. "But I liked it anyway. Thanks."

Morgan patted his cheek then held her arms out to Joe. He scooted over to claim her—thrilled she needed him the way he needed her—but sat close enough to acclimate her to having a man flanking her on both sides. He could practically feel the vibrations rolling off the three other men in the truck as they observed the pivotal exchange.

They might have doubted her, but Joe didn't.

Morgan wouldn't be intimidated by their hunger.

She would blossom under their attention, exactly as she had with him.

"Where are Kate and Mike?" she wondered aloud as she settled against his side. Her right hand lingered on Dave's thigh. Joe had always been closest to Dave. It pleased him to know Morgan felt so at ease with his friend. He met the other man's stare over Morgan's head and grinned at the latent passion lingering there.

"They left from the festival for their weekend away," James answered from the front with a waggle of his eyebrows Joe spotted in the rearview mirror.

"I think he has something special planned." Neil cleared his throat.

James slugged his partner in the shoulder. "Shut up. Don't spoil his secret."

"You would torture me like that all weekend? Come on, tell me." Morgan came awake further as her curiosity got the best of her.

"Oh, we'd torture you all kinds of ways this weekend, if you'd let us." The corner of Dave's mouth tipped up in a feral grin that had Joe's cock throbbing in his jeans.

Of course, his girl noticed.

"I see you like the idea." She rubbed the bulge behind Joe's zipper without a hint of subtlety. Neil didn't bother to hide his interest. He spun in his seat for a direct view.

"Almost as much as you do, I bet." Joe couldn't help but consume the smirk that appeared on her fallen-angel lips. When they broke apart, still panting, he asked, "Why don't you let Dave see how bad you want him?"

CHAPTER SIX

Morgan shivered beneath the weight of Joe's dare. The consequences could be far reaching. But she believed what he'd promised earlier in the evening. He would never tempt her with fantasies then resent her for taking what she dreamed of later.

He was no hypocritical bastard. He was no Craig.

Joe gave her a tiny nod.

She wormed her shoulders into the crook of his arm—braced against his chest—then spread her legs, draping one thigh over Dave's knee. She peeked up at him, then back to Joe.

Joe bent forward to kiss her again, long and thorough.

With his tongue lulling her into a dazed state of arousal, she didn't notice the fingers tracing her pussy through her jeans couldn't be his until they'd made several full passes along the length of the seam at her crotch. From their positioning, the romancing hands had to belong to Dave. The realization had her squirming. The top of her thighs glided across the denim encasing them, and her breasts ached in the confines of her bra.

"Shit, I can feel how wet she is through her clothes." Dave groaned. "Soaked."

Her eyelids fluttered open, and she turned to meet his heated stare head-on. No point in denying it now. God, how could she be so greedy? She'd already had the best night of her life.

Morgan rocked from side to side in the men's hold when they turned from the gravel farm road onto the paved highway. Occasional lights from vehicles passing the other direction whizzed past them in the darkness. Who was out this late at night?

They couldn't see inside the tinted windows, could they?

"Her nipples are hard too." Neil's usually smooth tone had gone rough. "Someone rub them. She needs you to touch her."

Dave's hand meandered beneath her sweater to cup her breast. True, the satin of her bra still separated them, but he applied pressure to the aching peaks. Morgan inclined her head until she could flash Neil a grateful smile. The testosterone whipping through the air around her made it impossible to speak.

Impossible to move.

Almost impossible to breathe.

"Holy shit." The truck swerved a little when James caught an eyeful in the rearview mirror. "That's hot."

"Show us your tits." The frank speech whipped her stare to Neil, her eyebrows climbing. She hadn't expected it from him. That'd teach her to underestimate the laid-back man.

"It's been a while since we've played with a woman." Though unnecessary, James offered an apology for his mate.

She swore the four men all held their breath. Having that much power over the experienced studs went straight to her head.

Before Morgan could balk, she shoved her sweater to her neck and shimmied her arms from the sleeves. She peeled the bra straps from her shoulders and wiggled the cups until her breasts popped free. They rested on the material—plumped, straining and utterly exposed.

Neil jammed his hand beneath the waistband of his well-worn jeans to cup his hard-on, a ragged groan testament to his approval. "I wish I could suck your nipples right now."

"I wish I could suck your cock right now." James moaned from beside his lover.

"Don't worry, you're going to have all you can handle when we make it home." His gentle caress on James's knee belied the strong statement.

The interplay between the men set Morgan on edge before they'd really started to explore. They had to be most of the way to her nearby apartment by now, didn't they? Shit, yes, they slowed for the four way stop a couple miles from the shop. What would happen when they reached it?

She had to come before the guys scattered for the night. Had to steal one taste of the forbidden if that were all she had the opportunity to try.

"Go ahead, cupcake," Joe whispered near her temple. "Ask for what you want. We'll grant you anything you need."

"I need to come. Please, Dave. Joe." Her head rocked on her lover's chest as his breath sawed in and out. "Make me come."

Dave ripped open her fly then shoved her pants to her knees. With little finesse, he sank his fingers inside her as far as he could reach. Exactly as she needed. Joe scooted to the front edge of their seat then focused on her chest. He pinched her nipples, squeezing them with rhythmic pulls that matched the tempo Dave set in her pussy.

A strangled moan from Neil's direction pushed her closer to the razor's edge of desire. How must she look?

Wanton.

Hedonistic.

Truly alive.

She closed her eyes and surrendered to the physical sensations the men inspired but none of them had the impact of the emotional mind-fuck their infatuation delivered. Thinking of the four sets of eyes on her shoved her to the brink.

The lap of Dave's tongue on her engorged clit sent her flying.

Morgan's scream of fulfillment cut short when Joe covered her parted lips, showing her with his wild kiss how much she'd affected him. She reached her hands out to either side, seeking blindly in her rapture, and latched onto the bulge in his pants. He thrust hard against her palm then stiffened.

"Fuck, yes," he growled. "Coming."

Dave didn't speak but his short series of grunts made it clear he'd achieved his own satisfaction. Every carnal sound sent another wave of pleasure zooming through her body until she would have begged for mercy or swore her heart would explode in the next second.

After what could have been seconds or minutes, she began to return to reality.

"Get your mouth on me. Quick." Neil's command cut through her desire. She watched as he buried his fingers in

James's sandy hair and tugged his boyfriend's mouth over the cock jutting from the open fly of his jeans.

Morgan hadn't realized they had parked at the foot of the wooden stairs leading up to the apartment above her bakery. How long had they been outside?

James's lips stretched to accommodate the proud length of his lover's cock. Thinner than Joe's hard-on, it had him in length by an inch or so. Impressive—and so fucking hot— James could take the whole thing down his throat. The instant his lips ringed the base of Neil's shaft, Neil fisted his hands at his side and groaned.

Morgan watched his balls tighten beneath his lover's chin. James's throat worked to swallow all of Neil's come but an opaque bead escaped the corner of his mouth and trickled onto the other man's trimmed pubic hair.

An echo of her orgasm contracted her pussy in an aftershock that squeezed more arousal from her slit. Dave responded by licking it from her in a never-ending spiral of lust and fulfillment. Part of something so intimate—by sharing that kind of elemental energy with these men—she felt larger than one person, more than one super-lucky woman who'd stumbled into a sexual exchange of colossal proportions.

Morgan felt connected.

She felt grounded.

Happy, for the first time in a long time.

"Better?" Joe caressed her face as he peered into her eyes in the wake of the destruction of all her preconceived truths.

"Phenomenal." She closed her eyes, completely exhausted, thoroughly relaxed, and remembered nothing until the next morning.

***

Morgan blinked, afraid of what she'd find when she opened her eyes.

She shouldn't have worried.

Joe lay on his side. He propped his head on one hand as he studied her with a grin, which bordered on silly, stretched across his handsome face. "Good morning, cupcake."

"Mmm...morning." She debated saying more, but didn't know where to start. He beat her to it.

"Morgan, I want you to know I didn't mean for the guys to come for us last night. I lost track of time. I didn't plan for any of that to happen in the truck. Not so soon, with things so new between us." His forehead dropped to hers until the bare honesty in his eyes consumed her field of vision. "But goddamn I loved every second of it. The way the crew looked at you, the sounds you made when Dave touched you, how fast you came on his hand and tongue, how much pleasure we gave you together. How much you returned. All of it."

"Oh God, me too." Slick juices wet her thighs at the memory. And they'd barely scratched the surface of the possibilities. "Joe?"

"Yeah, cupcake." He rose above her, the thick length of his shaft dropping onto her belly with a thud.

"It's my birthday." She gave him a slow, devious smile then shifted until her pussy kissed the head of his cock.

"And I think I have the perfect gift." His tongue dueled with hers as he plunged into her steaming core and drove all thoughts of anything more than this bond, this ecstasy, from her mind.

CHAPTER SEVEN

Morgan stepped from the shower into Joe's arms. He toweled her dry, paying special attention to her pussy and breasts until she laughed, grabbing the terry cloth from his rough hands. It still amazed her that he could touch her so gently with them.

He ducked into her closet while she wrapped her hair to dry. Alone with her reflection, she studied the various love bites he'd left last night and the more vivid ones from his ardent necking earlier this morning.

They'd spent the day together, exchanging stories about their past, things they hadn't discussed in the last several months—the things that had shaped them into the people they were today. People who seemed dangerously close to falling into something deeper than lust with each other. The more she learned, the more she cared and it seemed to work the same for him.

At least she hoped it did.

Joe broke her reverie when he dropped a kiss on her shoulder. His arm wrapped around her middle from behind. The band of dark, strong sinew against her pale belly in the mirror thrilled her. "You're so gorgeous like this. It's a crime to cover you up."

"I could say the same for you." She turned in his hold. "You have the most extraordinary body I've ever seen outside a movie. But you'll never be able to hide how attractive you are to me. Even with a parka and snow pants I'd still be able to see the man beneath. The man who turns me on with one look. The man I can talk to for hours..."

Could he actually blush?

Morgan could have sworn he planned to kiss her, maybe molest her on the bathroom floor, considering the careful distance they'd kept all afternoon. The brief abstinence had her strung tight, nearing her limit. Soon she would beg him to fuck her again.

She moaned then pressed closer.

Joe smacked her ass hard enough to sting before stepping back. He held up a simple yet sexy black dress she'd bought but never worn because it seemed so much more revealing in her apartment than it had in the store. "Put this on then meet me in the living room."

"Are we going somewhere?" She tried to hide her disappointment.

"It's a surprise. Get dressed, okay?"

"Yes, sir." Morgan chuckled when his pupils dilated.

"We'll have more time for those games later, cupcake. Then we'll see if you're still laughing...or begging for mercy."

She shivered then did as he requested, taking five minutes to blow dry her hair and apply a hint of makeup. The front door closed kind of hard, making more noise than usual since they'd left one of the windows open this afternoon.

With Joe nearby the autumn afternoon had seemed downright steamy.

Had he left?

"Joe?" Morgan traipsed into the kitchen, barefoot, to investigate.

Joe, Dave, Neil and James circled the countertop while Joe flicked a lighter, finally getting it to catch. She must have made a small sound when she realized they were putting candles on a birthday cake.

"Oops, I think our secret is out." James noticed her first.

"Surprise!" The guys pitched into an off-key rendition of the birthday song while Joe finished igniting the colorful wax sticks. Dave held out his hand as Joe tipped the cake toward her.

"Make a wish."

"I did, remember?" She grinned at the four men huddled around her. Neil rested his arm on her waist and Dave teased the locks of hair at her nape but she stared straight into the emerald depths of Joe's eyes. "And it already came true."

Morgan smiled at each of them as her gaze roamed among the four hot friends before she bent to extinguish the flames. "This cake looks familiar."

"I snagged it from the case downstairs." Joe looked sheepish for a minute. "Only the best for my girl."

Her heart stuttered and the other guys receded from her awareness for a moment. "Am I?"

"The best? Absolutely. My girl?" Joe grinned when she nodded. "God, I hope so."

Without thinking, she launched toward him, crashing into his side and knocking the cake off balance in his hand. Dave tried to avert disaster but the triple-layer, chocolate cake—

complete with strawberry filling that would be a bitch to get up without staining the tiles—skid sideways on the doily-covered cardboard round. It smooshed into the palm he'd thrust in the path of doomed dessert.

The motion kept it from crashing to the floor but it tore into pieces, glued together loosely with globs of icing. Jellied fruit oozed up from the center as though the cake were bleeding to death. "Oh crap, sorry!"

The guys only laughed.

"You baked the thing, you're entitled to ruin it," James supplied.

"Plus, who cares what it looks like. It'll still taste fucking great." Dave's gaze heated. "Just like everything else you make."

He shuffled toward the sink to rinse his hand but Joe stopped his friend with a light touch on the other man's elbow. "Wait, I have a better idea."

The wicked glint in his eyes had her taking a couple giant steps backward.

"Oh, no. No. Joe! This is a brand new dress."

"Then let's take it off so it doesn't get ruined. Cause, I promise, we're about to take the term feeding frenzy to a whole new level."

"I like the way you think." James sidled up behind her, trapping her between their work-hardened bodies. "Let me help."

When she pivoted her head to stare at him with bug eyes, he nodded reassurance then kissed her cheek. His fingertips teased the skin of her thighs at hem of her dress. He whispered, "I can stop if you're not ready."

Morgan didn't move.

She kept her stare locked on Joe while James stripped her slowly, revealing her by tiny degrees to his partners.

"Son of a bitch. I'm hungry." Neil shot his lover a dirty look. "Hurry, you tease."

James laughed but continued at his painfully slow pace. Joe still held the remnants of the cake, and Dave's hands were slathered in icing. Neil couldn't resist. He sank to his knees at her feet, running his palms up her calves, then her thighs.

"I wanted to touch you so bad last night." He nuzzled her mound when James revealed the lilac lace creating a flimsy barrier between them. "You're smoking hot."

It felt both odd and amazing to have someone other than Joe making contact with her skin. Another man's breath on her pussy. But the intensity of Joe's stare made it clear he enjoyed every moment, almost as much as she did. Knowing he watched heightened the arousal beginning to fire her blood. These four guys turned her on in ten seconds flat.

"I can smell how much you want us."

Morgan yelped when Neil licked the wet spot growing on her panties. "Screw the cake, I want to eat you."

"Soon," Joe interjected. "Finish getting her naked, then come help us. My zipper is about to leave permanent marks on my cock."

"You heard your guy." James nudged her arms until she raised them above her head. "Enough teasing."

He stripped her dress off then flicked open her bra with one smooth movement. Neil groaned, his lips drifting to her flat abdomen, his hands cupping her ass. When James revealed her breasts to his lover, Neil latched on to one of the mounds. His moan sent vibrations through the hardening nipple straight to her pussy.

"Nice," Dave moaned.

"Get rid of those panties," Joe barked at James.

James dropped to his knees beside Neil, who supported her with his big hands, which spanned her waist. James took the tip of her other breast into his mouth as he slipped his fingers beneath the elastic of her panties. Having two men sucking on her, together, had her crying out. She tangled her fingers in their hair, holding them tight to her.

When her panties fell to her ankles, she stepped out of them. The two men at her breasts molded the masses close together then rotated their heads. Their tongues slid all over her cleavage, her nipples and each other's lips. The lust they shared radiated out from where the men touched, catching her in the blast radius. Their ardor expanded within her, amplifying the desire already melting her inhibitions.

Morgan looked to Joe for help. She needed more.

"Bring her to the kitchen table." Joe broke through to the men feasting at her chest. Neil scooped her into his arms as he levered to his feet. She clung to his neck until he delivered her to the narrow, rectangular table in the center of her small breakfast nook. "Yes, lay her down."

Neil did as Joe directed.

The clear plastic covering over the antique surface made her gasp. The cool material contrasted with the intense heat of her primed body, which only rose in temperature when she realized James now knelt at Dave's feet. She didn't blink once as he used his teeth to rip open the button fly of Dave's jeans then reached inside to withdraw the other man's cock.

Neil kissed her cheek then moaned when Joe asked, "You like watching them together?"

"God, yes." Morgan's hand slid down her body, cupping her aching breast. "So sexy."

"Neil." Without another word, the man at her side spun toward Joe's call.

Her fingers slipped from her breast toward her pussy when the strong man obeyed her boyfriend. Neil sank to the ground in front of Joe. She couldn't help but run one finger beside her clit when masculine hands reached for Joe's zipper. Joe groaned as Neil relieved the pressure on his straining cock, freeing it from the confines of his jeans.

They made smoldering bookends. Joe and Dave stood, their messy hands outstretched, while Neil and James removed their pants and socks. Something about the exchange had Morgan's legs spreading farther apart. She inserted her index finger into her sopping pussy, amazed to feel how hot she was to the touch.

Nothing had turned her on like this before.

James and Neil cupped their friends' cocks and balls in their palms then stroked the rock-hard shafts from root to tip several times. The wet, fleshy sounds they made drew a moan from her. Joe looked up from where he and Neil intersected. His hips arched when he saw Morgan touching herself. The motion caused his cock to glide across

Neil's cheek, leaving a glistening smudge of pre-come behind. Neil swiped at it then brought his thumb to his mouth.

"Son of a bitch!"

Morgan wasn't sure who'd said it but she totally agreed.

When James took the head of Dave's cock into his mouth for a quick kiss she nearly came on the spot. Both men shared a look of rapture that she felt privileged to share.

"Hurry." Joe spurred the men to strip off his and Dave's shirts. "I have to be inside her. Soon."

The guys did the best they could with the icing, cake and jelly but some of those fingerprints would never come out. Morgan would buy them new clothes. It'd be well worth the price for the sight before her now.

Joe and Dave closed in on her, gloriously naked, while James and Neil stripped themselves faster than she would have imagined possible before joining them around the table. Joe set the ruined cake near her hip and smirked. He plastered his sloppy hands over her breasts then dragged them along her torso. Dave daubed her lips with the tip of one finger. She opened for him, sucking the chocolate from his knuckle until it was mostly clean. He followed Joe's lead, cupping her mound then smearing his palm upward until he'd transferred most of the sugary wreckage to her skin.

The crew descended on her like starving men. They devoured the gourmet confection from her nipples, navel and abdomen. Their tongues stimulated every nerve ending on her front side as they licked, sucked and nipped.

Morgan cried out with the intense pleasure of their attention. She folded her arms beneath her head for a better view, thrusting her breasts more firmly into their hold. When two of the men cleaned a spot near each other, they'd sometimes pause to enjoy a taste of their friend. Joe flicked his gaze to hers as he claimed James's mouth.

Something about the two men kissing drove her wild.

She squirmed beneath them, begging for someone to soothe the riot of ecstasy overtaking her pussy. As they removed the last of the icing from her breasts, they tracked lower and lower. Neil grabbed her hips and yanked so her ass perched on the very edge of the table. He kicked out the chair there and sat.

Joe and Dave each took hold of one of her thighs and spread her wide open. She glanced down her center until she met the dark blue of Neil's penetrating stare.

"Please," she begged.

He growled as he covered her pussy with his open mouth. He lapped at her cream, which mingled with the chocolate coating her. Her entire body tensed, poised on the edge of climax after less than a dozen bold swipes of his clever tongue.

The four men overwhelmed her senses.

Morgan reached for Joe, unable to put into words the rapture shooting like fireworks in her brain. Her hand closed around his cock and squeezed, drawing his attention to her plight.

"Oh shit, she's close already."

Neil groaned then redoubled his efforts. He ate her as though she were the sweetest treat on earth.

The bulging cock in her hand felt so good, she reached for Dave on her other side. Both men pumped into her fists, grunting and cursing beneath their breath as they witnessed their friend devouring her. The table shook a little, and she looked up to see James kneeling by her head.

"Doesn't seem right for the birthday girl to go without cake." His grin looked more like a grimace as need twisted it into something feral.

"Feed me," she moaned her permission.

James dug into the remaining cake and slathered his cock with delectable goo. She opened wide as he guided his erection to her eager mouth. Neil zeroed in on a particularly sensitive spot on her pussy, making her moan around his lover's cock.

"Oh shit, yeah. Right there, Neil," James panted as he drove between her lips. "Don't stop."

Whether he spoke to her or Neil she couldn't say but she didn't plan on letting James go anytime soon, and she prayed Neil had similar inclinations. Joe shouted when her fingers wrapped tighter around him. He and Dave continued to fuck her fists as they played with her chest and kept her open for Neil. When the men's gazes clashed they leaned forward and shared a ferocious kiss.

Morgan shifted her attention when James groaned, though the image of that moment would be etched in her memory forever. She worked her way lower on James's shaft, cleaning him as she went. Though still impressive, he was smaller than the other guys. She appreciated that fact as she took him to the root, swallowing around him.

"Oh God." He went still above her.

"You see that, Neil?" Joe taunted them all. "Your guy is about to blow in record time. He's going to shoot down Morgan's throat."

She knew it was a warning but she didn't care. Instead, she sucked James harder, rubbing her tongue across the sensitive underside of his hard-on. The moment the first jet of come landed on her palette Neil embedded several fingers in her pussy. The combination of his expert manipulations had her joining James in climax.

Morgan strangled the digits inside her as she gulped around James's cock, swallowing every last drop of his release. She didn't realize he'd finished coming until the world returned to focus, and he withdrew his softening member from between her lips.

"Magnificent," he whispered against her mouth then kissed her, slow and gentle. In the aftermath of her orgasm, the soft touch brought her alive again. How long they made out for, she couldn't say. But, soon, she sought the cocks that had so recently filled her grip. The men had stepped back to watch, stroking their own solid hard-ons.

James stumbled away. He dragged the chair Neil had abandoned to the side of their makeshift stage for an optimal view then collapsed into it. Neil stood between her legs now, his erection full and ruddy. "Please, let me fuck you."

The raw longing in his voice fanned her arousal. Joe looked to her for confirmation. She nodded. He tossed a condom from a pile on the counter, which she hadn't noticed before, in Neil's direction.

He ripped it open and sheathed himself in record time.

Joe advanced, to stand beside her. He halted a hairsbreadth away then whispered, "I love seeing you like this. Open. Needy. Honest. Unbelievably fucking sexy."

She moaned into his mouth when he kissed her. Unlike James, he kissed her hard. His tongue delved into the recesses of her mouth. She wondered if he could taste the cake there, or his friend's semen. The possibility had her shivering with anticipation.

The tip of Neil's covered cock nudged her pussy. Her hips rocked instinctively.

Joe separated from her just enough for her to watch as his friend penetrated her for the first time.

"Oh Christ!" Neil scrunched his eyes closed. "There's no way I'm going to last."

He moved inside her, slow for the first couple of passes but quickly gaining steam. He fucked her with strong strokes that jiggled her breasts every time he filled her. Joe stayed close, whispering dirty talk. Telling her over and over how much he loved watching her secure pleasure from his friends.

Morgan's desire rebuilt, though not as rapidly as Neil's. He rode her hard now, fucking with intense motions of his hips that even her recently sated pussy couldn't ignore. Dave groaned then reached for the top of her slit. His fingers honed in on her clit as though he'd touched her a million times before. Neil's pelvis tapped Dave's hand with every circuit, causing his fingers to bounce and grind on her engorged clit.

"Yes!" She forced her eyes to stay open and drink in the sight of the men arousing themselves, each other and her.

When Neil's cock bulged inside her and his strokes grew jerky, James rose from his seat. He stood behind his lover, kissing Neil's shoulders and neck while his hand caressed the defined muscles of Neil's sweaty chest on the way to playing with his nipples.

Neil didn't seem to be able to resist the dual assault. His head dropped onto James's shoulder, and he shuddered as he emptied himself into the condom he wore. The sight of his surrender ratcheted her arousal higher. The moment Neil began to go soft in her and withdrew, she writhed on the table. Her sweltering gaze met Joe's.

"You." She couldn't quite catch her breath. "I need you. Buried deep. Now."

Joe groaned then glanced toward Dave. She squinted at her boyfriend's best friend and saw what Joe did. The tendons in Dave's neck stood out as he practically strangled his cock in his white-knuckled grip. He wasn't going to endure much longer.

"We could fuck her together." Dave's gruff suggestion hung in the air.

"Have you ever been fucked in the ass?" Joe petted the stray wisps of hair from her face.

"No." She grimaced.

"And you're not really into the idea." Even Dave could see through her brave face. "No worries, love. Each of us has our limits."

"You can fuck me." James turned in Neil's arms to face Dave. "It's been a while."

"Can we try something else first?" Morgan couldn't believe she'd spoken up. Her face flamed.

All four men seemed to take a step closer, eager to hear her suggestion. "Can't I take you both..."

She still had *some* shyness. She looked away.

But the crew knew what she meant.

"Fuck, yes." Joe plucked her from the table, enfolding her in his arms. He kissed her while Dave grabbed a condom from the counter and rolled it on.

James gathered the remaining crumbles of cake and transferred them to the sink as best he could. Dave hopped onto the table, reclining on his back. His cock pulsed, bobbing from where it lay on his abdomen. He collared the base with his fingers until it stood out perpendicular from his torso.

Joe deposited her on the table, placing her on her knees facing Dave's feet. With one hand, he guided his best friend's cock to her pussy. When it aligned with her opening, she sank onto her haunches, swallowing Dave to the root.

An unintelligible moan sounded below her. Dave's fists pounded the table as she bowed, working him inside her fully. His toes curled at the end of the table.

Joe leaned on the furniture, testing his weight, but the solid oak didn't even tremble. He crawled between her and Dave's spread legs, pressing her to her back in the process. The full-body contact with Dave's hard muscles and heated skin scorched her. He reached around to cup her breasts, teasing the nipples with light flicks while Joe got situated.

"Tell me if this hurts." He stared into her eyes without moving until she bestowed her promise.

Then he traced the thick vein on the underside of Dave's cock with his flared head until it led him straight to the heart of her pussy. He held his shaft down with two fingers, squeezing in beside his friend.

"Oh my God," she screamed at the ultra-fullness pervading her pussy. The swollen tissue stretched. The oversensitive walls simultaneously rebelled and craved more. Joe inched in further, fucking both her and Dave with tiny hitches of his hips. More than half of his length embedded in her.

"I think that's as far as I can go." His forehead rested on hers as he ravished her lips. "So fucking tight."

Dave groaned below them. "Fuck. Need you to move. Fuck her. Fuck us."

Joe needed it too. Morgan could see his fervor in the set of his jaw and the tension in his shoulders. Trapped between two infernos, she couldn't help but catch on fire.

Joe locked his elbows, hovering over her in an obscene version of a push up. He began to rock inside her, tentative at first. Every time he shifted, all three of them moaned.

James and Neil observed from between their legs at the foot of the table. James groaned at the sight. "It's like you're stroking Dave's balls with your cock, Joe."

"I bet that feels un-fucking-believable," Neil muttered with envy.

"Does." Dave shuddered beneath her. "Harder, Joe."

He looked to Morgan for confirmation.

"Do it." She cried out when he thrust in deep. "I can't take much more."

"She's stretched so tight around you." Neil and James kept a running commentary, making all three of them suffer as they strained toward the promise of pleasure greater than any they'd known before.

The table rocked when Joe began to really pump inside her. Dave grabbed her hips and thrust from below. The two cocks inside her rubbed and slipped against each other. Morgan stopped thinking and lost herself in a universe comprised only of senses— the feel of them fucking her into oblivion, the sound of their grunts and moans, the smell of their arousal mixed with the lingering flavor of the chocolate cake.

All of it combined to detonate a violent reaction. Before she could say anything, before she could even prepare herself, her orgasm crashed through her. She convulsed arounda the men fucking her, dragging them with her in a shared release of epic proportions. Dave stiffened first, filling the condom inside her with pulse after pulse of come.

Her climax continued to drown her with waves of pure pleasure. Joe breathed a lungful of air into her constricted chest as he blew out a massive sigh, ending on a strangled groan. Hot jets of semen burst from his cock, splattering into the depths of her pussy and coating the latex barrier between them and Dave.

His orgasm seemed to drag on for hours, just as hers did.

And then the world faded to black.

When she recovered, Morgan was cradled in Joe's arms on the floor of her shower. Warm water began to cascade over them but neither had the energy to make a move for the soap.

"Welcome back, cupcake."

"Hi." She kissed his neck.

"How do you feel?" Joe's question sounded scratchy from the strain of his earlier shouts.

"Never better." She lay boneless in his grip. "You?"

She held her breath. It was the moment of truth. How would he feel now that they'd acted out the fantasy?

How weird would things be?

"Sublime. But I think we've only just begun, Morgan." He smiled against her damp hair. "Happy birthday."

Grateful for the droplets of water beading on his chest, she let the moisture seep from the corners of her eyes. The happiest tears she'd ever shed.

EPILOGUE

Sunday evening had arrived far too fast. The best weekend of Morgan's life was now history, though she would bet there were plenty more coming to rank high on her list. She ran past the crew, as they lounged on her couch, studying the sports highlights on TV, to answer a familiar knock at her door.

"You're back." She saquashed Kate in a fierce hug. If it hadn't been for her best friend, none of this would have happened. But, before she could drag the woman somewhere private to dish, she caught the look on Kate's face. "Wow, even happier than when you left. I didn't think that was possible."

Kate wiggled the fingers of her left hand in front of Morgan's nose. A high-pitched double-squee turned four heads from the living room. Mike covered his ears then squeezed past the women as they bounced and giggled some more. The glow of Kate's smile nearly matched the glint from her gorgeous diamond ring.

"I'm so happy for you. Truly." Morgan hugged her best friend until she squeaked. "But..."

"What?" Kate angled her head.

Morgan grimaced at the shadow dimming her friend's enthusiasm. "Nothing. Sorry—"

"No, please. Don't do that. Tell me what you're really thinking."

"It's just..." Morgan lowered her voice then peeked over Kate's shoulder to where Joe leaned his hip against the counter. The crew took turns slapping Mike on the back and offering their congratulations. "Isn't this all sort of quick? You've only known him a few months. How do you know it'll last?"

As though he could sense her stare, Joe turned. Their eyes met, and his gaze intensified. A corresponding thrill ran through her veins. Could this be the real thing? A forever-after kind of love?

How could it not be?

"You knew Craig all your life. But deep down, you understood it would never last," Kate whispered. "It's kind of like that, but opposite. When he's the one, you know. Time doesn't matter."

Joe winked then held out his hand as though their thirty seconds apart had seemed as long to him as it did to her. She ached to feel his fingers surrounding hers, sheltering her with their calloused strength.

Without him, she felt incomplete.

"You're right." Morgan hugged Kate one more time. "Congratulations."

"Right back at you. Looks like you had a busy weekend."

The women laughed as they rejoined the crew in the other room. Joe's arm came around Morgan's shoulder, welcoming her into the heat and laughter they all shared.

It felt perfect.

And she knew.

WHAT HAPPENS TO JOE AND
THE REST OF THE CREW? KEEP
READING TO FIND OUT!

KAYLA'S GIFT

POWERTOOLS

JAYNE RYLON

NEW YORK TIMES BESTSELLING AUTHOR

One blizzard, two days, three men to keep her warm.

Naked is Kayla's style. She's exposed to bare skin more than the average person—like when she's up to her elbows in massage oil, soothing the tired muscles of the construction crew building her new spa, a barter to offset some of the cost. Once it's finished, she plans to open a private retreat for fellow naturists.

It should be a routine service. Yet for some reason, caressing the man on her table is blurring her normally crystal-clear distinction between nudity and sexuality. And stirring up kinky fantasies involving the rest of the crew.

She never intended to share details about her lifestyle-slash-business plan, not even with the open-minded, sexy crew. But when a faulty truck engine and one hell of a snowstorm trap the three men at her cabin, heat sears away her cover story—and her inhibitions.

Cocooned in blissful isolation, Dave, Neil and James show her that passion knows no barrier, with or without clothing. Leaving Kayla wondering if two days of mutual satisfaction will ever be enough…

Warning: This book features a m/m/m/f ménage hot enough to melt an entire blizzard's worth of snow and ice.

EXCERPT FROM KAYLA'S GIFT, POWERTOOLS BOOK 3

"Hey, you okay?"

She blinked. When had Dave moved? He dragged faded denim over his lean hips. Damn it. She licked her lips as he tugged on a thin gray T-shirt, which obscured his firm pecs, then his six-pack and finally the ridge caused by his inguinal ligament—her absolute favorite spot on a man's body. She could lick the crest it created from his hip straight to his...

"Kayla?" Dave rested his broad hand on her elbow, shaking her from the daydream.

Shit! For a woman considering founding a naturist haven, she certainly had a hard time separating this man's form from his radiant attractiveness. A problem she'd never had before.

"Change your mind about staying? You can bunk with me if you're not interested in plugging your ears to block out the soundtrack accompanying all the sex rocking Mike and Kate's apartment."

She laughed. "Nah, I'm good. Ready for a couple quiet days, that's all."

"You're not sleeping enough."

No kidding. If she didn't order supplies, build a website, draft design concepts and secure the funding remaining to fill the gap after her sibling's generous contributions, who would?

"Yes, Dad."

"Fuck. Sorry. It's none of my business—"

"If her friends can't tell it like it is, who can?" Another heckler waltzed in on their conversation.

"James." She hugged Dave in a quick, silent apology as the slighter man neared. "You're right. Both of you. I promise to take a little time off to enjoy the season. You know, frolic in the snow and crap."

"Damn straight you will." Neil joined them in the suddenly cramped area. How had it seemed spacious to her before? "Not much else you'll be able to accomplish anyway. It's turning nasty."

Kayla ushered them out of her living room and onto the front porch, crossing her arms over her chest to ward off the intense chill. It could be a hundred below yet she'd rather endure the sting of the wind for a couple seconds than add another layer of clothing to her frame.

The more she went nude, the more it stifled her to be dressed. The holidays she'd spent with her family had driven her insane with discomfort. A few moments longer and she could retreat to the bliss of her fireplace.

Dave tugged on his leather jacket while the other two men piled into their beast of a truck.

"Drive safe."

Now that the guys prepared to pull out of her yard, a rebellious fraction of her mind wished she'd accepted Dave's offer. Several days without their easy company seemed like an awfully long time. How could that be when she'd only met them six weeks earlier?

"We will." He buttoned the flattering coat, inspiring a gulp.

She'd never seen him wear the thing before, never mind fasten it to the neck. Sporting something so constricting would suffocate her. Still, she wouldn't complain about the extra time his actions granted them.

"Call if you need anything, baby."

Like a hot construction worker to keep me toasty? Hopping from foot to foot to prevent her toes from numbing—still preferable than stuffing them into the prison of heavy shoes—she indulged her stubborn streak, which refused to abandon the porch until he'd vanished from sight. She chaffed her arms. Snowflakes swirled around them, drifting onto her hair. When one landed on her bottom lip, she licked the miniature puddle it left behind.

Dave's eyes slitted a moment before he growled, "Forget this."

Kayla gasped between his parted lips when he swooped in to taste the moisture for himself. The kiss caught her completely off guard. He hadn't telegraphed a single hint he'd noticed the electricity arcing between them.

Not once had he taken their flirtation beyond harmless.

Until now.

She sank into his loose hold.

His tongue stole its first taste of her mouth. The gust of passion he inspired knocked her off balance. She wrapped her arms around his neck to keep from losing her footing. When she thought she might try to crawl up him right there at the top of her stairs, in plain sight of his best friends, he retreated with a sigh.

Dave stroked wisps of hair from her cheek. "You'd better head in before you catch a chill."

"As though I could have a cool molecule left on my body." She touched her lips with her fingertips. "What was that?"

"I think it's called a kiss." He laughed.

"Jesus. Not hardly. I've kissed plenty of guys before."

Dave frowned.

"None of them fired me up like that. Amazing."

"How about we work on it some more after the storm?"

She couldn't speak so she nodded instead.

"Call me, Kayla. Let's talk."

"Promise."

Dave pivoted and leapt down the stairs, grinning at her over his shoulder as he loped to the truck. If Neil had pressed his face any closer to the driver's side window for a peep at the exchange, he'd have left a nose print on the glass. The instant he spotted his friend approaching, he turned the key in his truck's ignition.

The powerful engine roared.

Then it sputtered.

Right before it died.

ABOUT THE AUTHOR

Jayne Rylon is a *New York Times* and *USA Today* bestselling author. She received the 2011 RomanticTimes Reviewers' Choice Award for Best Indie Erotic Romance.

Her stories used to begin as daydreams in seemingly endless business meetings, but now she is a full-time author, who employs the skills she learned from her straight-laced corporate existence in the business of writing. She lives in Ohio with two cats and her husband, the infamous Mr. Rylon.

When she can escape her purple office, Jayne loves to travel the world, SCUBA dive, take pictures, avoid speeding tickets in her beloved Sky and—of course—read.

Printed in Great Britain
by Amazon

87603938R00086